Blue Looks for Books

Published by Advance Publishers, L.C.
www.advance-publishers.com

©2000 Viacom International Inc. All rights reserved. Nickelodeon,
Blue's Clues and all related titles, logos and characters are trademarks
of Viacom International Inc.
Visit Blue's Clues online at www.nickjr.com

S.E.A.L SOUTH
1265 Napervile Drive
Unit D
Romeoville, IL 60446

Written by K. Emily Hutta
Art layout by Niall Harding
Art composition by David Maxey, Brad McMahon, and Sheena Needham
Produced by Bumpy Slide Books

ISBN: 1-57973-082-5

Blue's Clues Discovery Series

Hi! Have you been waiting long? Oh, good.
We just got here, too.
    Blue and I were at the library.
It was kind of a special trip, actually.
    You see, it was Blue's first
visit there.

We borrowed some great books, didn't we, Blue? I wonder where we should put them so they don't get lost. On the bed? No. In the refrigerator? Uh-uh.

Oh. Maybe we can put them on top of the bookcase for now? Yeah!

There! Thanks for helping me put the books away.

So Blue, what should we do now? You want to make something to use with your books? What do you want to make?

Oh! We can play Blue's Clues to figure out what Blue wants to make to use with her books! Will you help us? You will? Great!

Hi, Blue! What have you got there? A book about fish. Cool!

Hey, I have an idea. Let's see what kinds of books our friends like to read. We can start with Tickety.

Hey, Tickety is reading a counting book. Cool!
What's that? You see a clue? Good job!
What is it? Oh. It's the page of that book.
Hmmm. So what do you think a page has to do
with what Blue wants to make?

Do you think we need more clues? Yeah, me too.

Hi, Slippery! What are you reading?

I'm reading a bath book. It's made of plastic so it can get wet in the tub.

A bath book, huh? Cool!

Hi, Mr. Salt and Mrs. Pepper. It sure smells good in here!

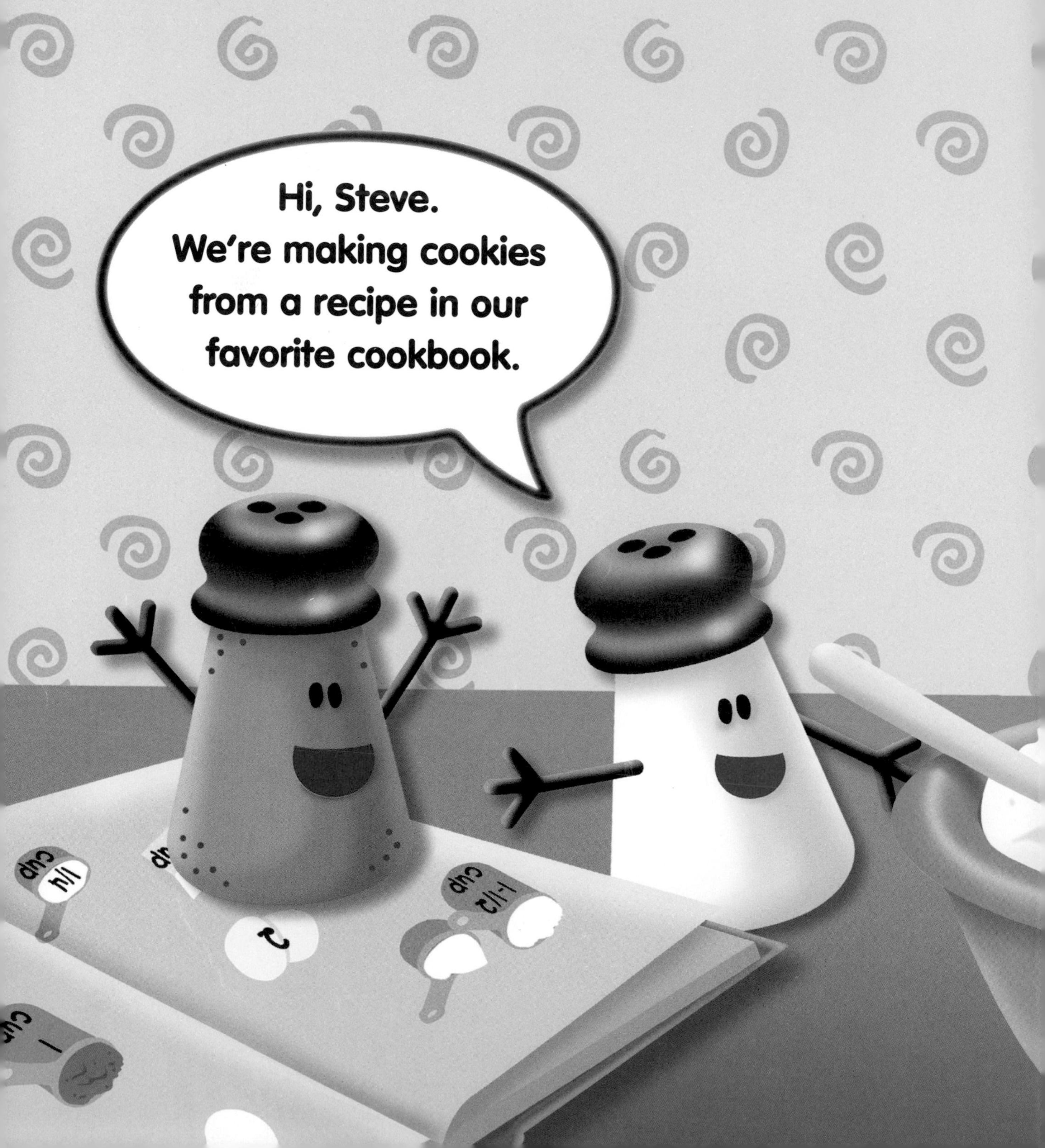

A cookbook! Yeah! Slippery likes bath books and you two like cookbooks!

Hey, look! Paprika has a book, too!

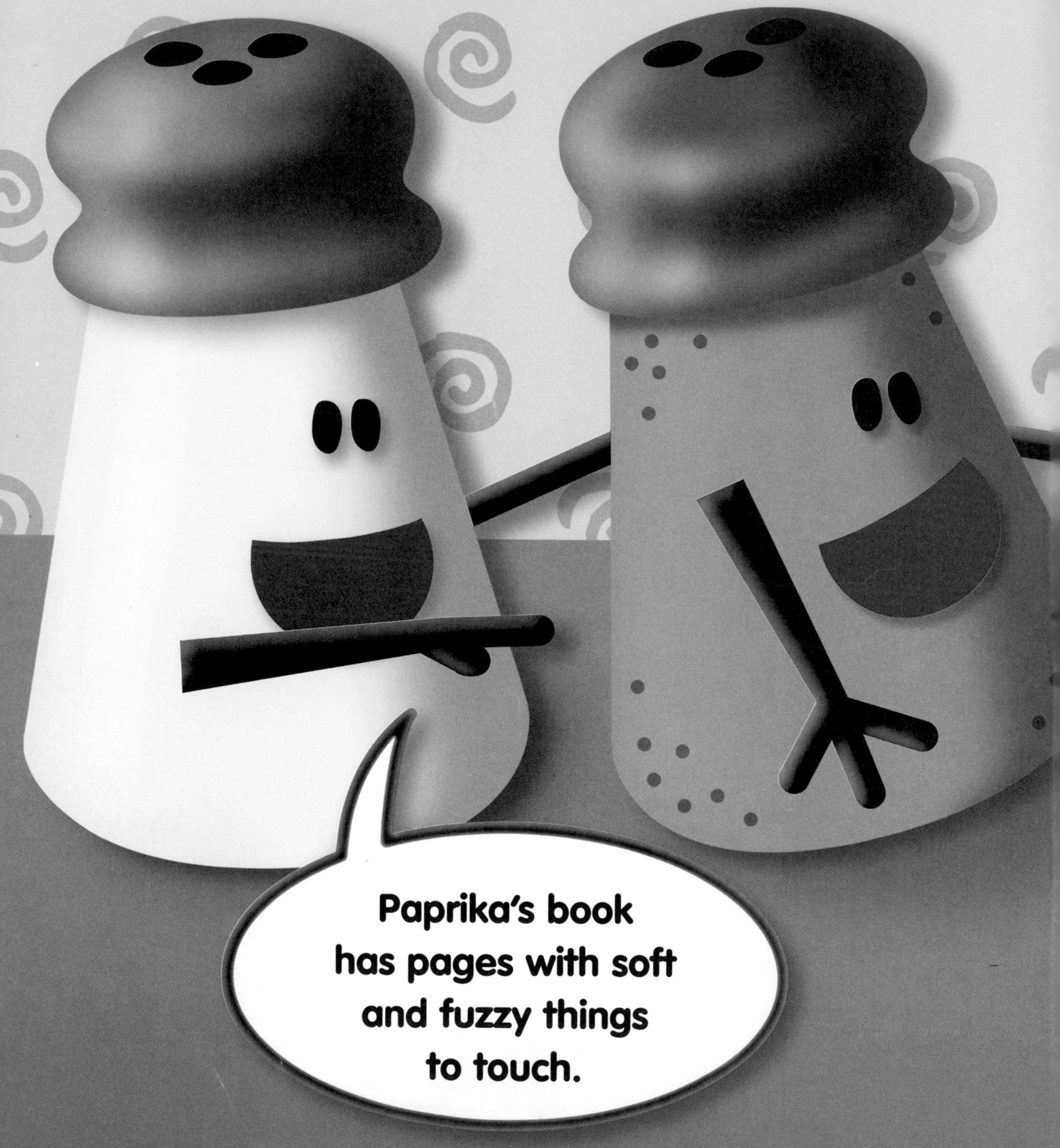

A book you can read and feel. What a great book! Thanks for showing us, Paprika.

Hey! Want to check out the living room for other kinds of books? You do? Oh! You see a clue on the art table.

It's a rectangular piece of cardboard. So our clues are a page and a rectangular piece of cardboard. Hmmm. I think we need to find our last clue.

Blue's found another kind of book. That's our phone book. I can tell because of that picture of the phone on the front.

Hey, what do you think those other books are about?

I'll just put these books back where they belong. What's that?

You see a clue? Oh! It's a tassel. That's our third clue!

You know what that means, don't you? It's time to go to our . . . Thinking Chair!

So our clues are a page, a piece of cardboard, and a tassel. What do you think Blue wants to make to use with a book?

That's it! Blue wants to make a bookmark to use with our books! We just figured out Blue's Clues! Thanks for all your help today. So long!

BLUE'S BOOKMARK BUDDY

You will need: 6" of grosgrain ribbon, one short pipe cleaner, craft glue, scissors, and bits of different colored felt

1. Starting at the top, cover 1" of the ribbon with craft glue.

2. Lay pipe cleaner across the ribbon, about 1/2" from the top.

3. Fold the top of the ribbon down to where glue ends, pressing securely.

4. Have a grown-up cut out eyes, a nose, and a mouth from the felt. Glue face in place.

5. Enjoy your new bookmark!